A KNIGHT IN TARNISHED ARMOR

A Knight in Tarnished Armor
Copyright © 2023 by David Oldakowski

Published in the United States of America
ISBN   Paperback: 978-1-959761-13-6
ISBN   eBook: 978-1-959761-14-3

All rights reserved. No part of this publication may be reproduced, stored in a retrieval system or transmitted in any way by any means, electronic, mechanical, photocopy, recording or otherwise without the prior permission of the author except as provided by USA copyright law.

The opinions expressed by the author are not necessarily those of ReadersMagnet, LLC.

ReadersMagnet, LLC
10620 Treena Street, Suite 230 | San Diego, California, 92131 USA
1.619. 354. 2643 | www.readersmagnet.com

Book design copyright © 2023 by ReadersMagnet, LLC. All rights reserved.

Cover design by Ericka Obando
Interior design by Daniel Lopez

A KNIGHT IN TARNISHED ARMOR

BY
DAVID CARL OLDAKOWSKI

ReadersMagnet, LLC

Dedication

*In loving memory of my Dad, Richard Carl Oldakowski,
who died proud of me for publishing this book.
And to my wonderful mother, without whose encouragement
this book would have probably never been submitted.*

11/10/14

READY FOR WAR

Music and Lyrics by Ean Leppin

G   C
Tarnished armor is what I've got.
G   C
Slaying dragons I cannot
Em   C
Hope is what I have been looking for
G   C
But my true need is what I ignore

G   C
Needing a shield to defend me from
G   C
Flaming arrows that continue to come
Em   C
All my strength is now leaving me
G   C
Needing a change but I can't pay the fee

Am   D
So I stand in this field of doubt
Am   D
Thirsty for a life giving fount

Chrous
              G   C
Lord give me – Boots that will stand in these evil days
              G   D
Give me – a helmet that will save my soul
              G   C
Give me – A sword with the sharpness of your word
        G   C
Jesus lead me on – I'm ready for war.

     G   C
Be the boldness in how I speak
        G   C
Be the love as I serve the meek
        Em   C
Be the strength and victory I'm fighting for
     G   C
Je-sus – I'm ready for war

Listen to the song on YouTube by searching for Ready For War (Tarnished Armor)

A Blessed and Happy Man

It's a cloudy Sunday morning But I don't have the blues
Without any kind of warning And no apparent clues
I'm a peaceful, happy man You see, once the sun has risen
We'll hardly know it's there
I'm about to leave this prison So really I don't care
I'm a grateful, happy man
It's gonna be kind of hazy With muggy, searing heat
Though the world outside's gone crazy I walk on steady feet
I'm a sober, happy man
There's a real likely chance of rain
And showers all day long
But I've a life of love to gain
And God has healed me strong
I'm a blessed and happy man!

David Oldakowski

A Brighter Morrow

I see so much pain and suffering and death
I see vanquished souls with nothing left
I see starving children everywhere
And homeless people with an empty stare
Into my heart this sadness spears
And I find myself awash in tears
I cry for the condition of this world
As well as for the death of my girl
For all whose pain I cannot ease
And I cry for victims of disease
To love, indeed, is to know sorrow
Yet still I pray for a brighter morrow

A Knight Fit to Fight

I will not build my house on the sand
Nor shall I cast my pearls before the swine
But I will travel throughout our land
And shall treat all people as friends of mine
I will not sit down with evil men
Nor shall I go into a den of thieves
But where I see evil, there and then
You can damn-well bet I'll roll up my sleeves!
No, you won't see me turning a cheek
Unless it's to get a kiss from my wife
God did not build me frail and weak
To turn my face from injustice in life
Where I see wrong doing I do act And where ere
I see evil I do fight
And I stake my life upon the fact
As God is my witness, I am a knight!

A Man without a Dog

Every night I brought her flowers when I came home from work. They weren't very expensive, but she loved me so much that it didn't matter anyway.
Every night she would faithfully have dinner prepared for us. She wasn't a real good cook, but I loved her so much that it didn't matter anyway.
Every night we would watch a little T.V. to keep us up to date on current events in our world. Then we would talk about our day, and honestly listen to each other. Sometimes we would take turns reading aloud a good book together when we finally went to bed. But always we would hug and kiss each other and usually wind up making love. But before we made love I would have to walk my dog. You see, we had a routine,
sand I loved my dog very much, too.
Sometimes she complained that I loved my dog too much, even that I loved my dog more than I loved her. She would even say, "Why couldn't I have ended up with a man with- out a dog?" Still, every night before we made love, I would have to walk my dog.

*Well, after only a year, my walking the dog really
became an issue when, one night,
already naked and ready to make love,
I got out of bed, got dressed and went out to walk my
dog. I won't tell you what she said to me that night!
By the time I returned and got back into bed,
she was already asleep. It was the first time she
had ever gone to sleep angry with me. So,
I realized it was time to tell her the truth.
The next night, after I had walked my dog,
I told her that the reason
I always walked my dog before we made love
was so that I could pass the gas from dinner,
as I would never want to do so
under the covers while we were making love.
Well she was so touched by this that she actually cried a bit.
She told me that I was the kindest, sweetest, most
thoughtful man she had ever known,
and that she would love me forever and ever!
That night we made love like never, ever before!
Well now, ever since she died and went on up to Heaven,
I selfishly pray that, no matter what,
God will never let her meet up with a man without a dog!*

David Oldakowski

A Place for You in Heaven

*You're the prettiest girl that
I've ever seen I feel so blessed that you exist
And to know that I am part of you
Brings tears of joy I can't resist
I love to be still and gaze at your picture
As it makes me feel like you're here with me
Not being able to see your face in
Heaven Is what my only fear would be
No, you were not made for this world alone
I simply cannot and will not believe it
So each night I pray for you a place in
Heaven And I've faith that God will surely receive it*

A Talk with My Beer

Oh, you, golden carbonated demon from hell
I ask myself why it is that I like you so well.
You sit there so casually staring back at me Knowing that if I
drink you, you will set me free
Free from all my worries and free from all my stress Free to
cast aside all things that are meaningless
Like grief and pity and useless empty dreams
And all those things of which true living really means
Now, I shall pick you up and drink you
And pray I'll be okay And if God sees fit to punish me
I'll live to drink another day

David Oldakowski

A Thousand Souls

A thousand souls have held mine hand
And come to help me understand
That life is here to live today
And that there lives no yesterday
There's no tomorrow till we find
Some way to leave the past behind
There are reasons for the pain we feel
And only time will have us to heal
Yet, if it is a seed which makes the flower
What then is time without the hour?
For, we build our dreams from broken glass
Whilst all things only come to pass
Then once we've done our very best
We leave for God to do the rest
Hence I gave my heart up to the sky
And beckoned God to hear my cry
They saw me standing there alone
A thousand souls beside mine own

I'll know contentment when I'm dead
A thousand souls to me hath said
So, though I hold my voyages' end draws near
To die I have no fret, no fear
Yea dying it is my dearest dream
For hence the truth I shall redeem!

David Oldakowski

All We Have Left

I've sailed the seas of loneliness
Lost anchor in the midst of tempest's swells
I've surmounted summits of eagerness
And died in valleys where sorrow dwells —
Healing my wounds in the desert's dark
I've cried out to God in my vision-quest
I met kindred spirits in fire's spark
And God did answer my dire request —
I've not yet kissed the lips of my wife
Nor conceived our child within her womb
It's all I've left to succeed in my life
Before I retire my flesh to the tomb —
I've climbed the jagged rocks of mountains
And looked through the eyes of the eagle's view
I've tasted the water from the fountains That makes us
envision our lives all a-new — I've struggled most of my life
away Corrupted by fear and money and doubt
Yet, God has told me that forth from this day
No longer love shall I do without —

ANOINTED AND APPOINTED

As I sit astride my trusted steed
A noble knight sworn to my quest
Until I vanquish evil's greed
My mortal body shall not rest
I'm an anointed soldier of the Lord
Waging war against all sin
An appointed opponent of discord
Raging battle deep within
Now, I've seen the mountains of my dreams
With snow capped peaks and crystal streams
I've strolled the meadows of honey blond hair
Loved in lush valleys and sown seed there
I've weathered great storms and come ashore wet
Then lived on islands of deep regret
I'm an anointed soldier of the
Lord Waging war against all sin
An appointed opponent of discord
Raging battle deep within
I've sought shelter in forests from the rain
And lived among people who were insane
I've scaled the cliffs of life's distrust
And wandered deserts eating dust

David Oldakowski

I've stayed my course forty-six long years
Through labor, yearning, blood, sweat and tears
Faceless foes have fallen by my sword
And I have championed my sovereign Lord!
I'm an anointed soldier of the Lord
Waging war against all sin
An appointed opponent of discord
Raging battle deep within
As I sit astride my trusted steed
A noble knight sworn to my quest
Until I vanquish evil's greed
My mortal body shall not rest!

ARTWORK OF LOVE

The art of my love Is the love of my art
And I digress not In its creation
For, love is the sum Of my soul and my heart
And bears no need of Interpretation
My body's a castle My heart is a throne In and upon which
My Savior doest reign
Hence no more forever Shall I walk alone
And no burden is more Than I can sustain
You're welcome to join me Here in my heart
Where my artwork of love Is on display
The art of my love Is the love of my art
Much like the potter As He works His clay
A gallery inspired By the Lord above
You're welcome to see The artwork

Of my love —

David Oldakowski

AT YOUR FEET

Your north-Atlantic, arctic-blue eyes, Have come to make me realize – That I could fall there-in so deep Where-in your soul your secrets keep – Whenever you are silent,
You make me wonder what you're thinking – Your mannerism is so gentle
Like a cautious gazelle as it's drinking – Yet, when you speak, I find myself, Anxiously clinging to all your words – And the depth of your emotion,
Is as strong as bison in their herds – Suffice to say that you, my dear, Are captivatingly complete –
And with my words I hope you hear That I've laid my virtue at your feet! –

Autumn Leaves

When Autumn came with summer's going
And turned the leaves into their gold
They changed without their ever knowing
That by their youth they'd now grown old
Then one by one they began to fall
Landing softly upon the ground
Paying tribute unto nature's call
They lay there still, without a sound
When Autumn left as the winter came
Taking with it a huge part of me
I felt such deep and sweet-bitter shame
For having stained her artistry
Then one by one I counted losses
Instead of all that I had gained –
No matter what the final cost is
My love for Autumn still remains
When winter came with Autumn's going
I felt the rain begin to freeze
And all at once it started snowing
And I fell down upon my knees
Then one by one the snowflakes gathered
Six feet high from top to bottom

David Oldakowski

I realized then that all that mattered
Was the blissful love I shared with Autumn
If I should love another Autumn
And feel the fear of falling leaves
I'll ask the Lord about my
Autumn What will I do if Autumn leaves?

BE WHERE YOU STAND

When yesterday's all you have,
And tomorrow seems way out of reach
Try to step off your chosen path,
And take a walk along the beach
Now, feel the sand between your toes,
The warmth of the sun upon your face
As you watch the waves come and go,
So do all us the human race
All our pasts are now behind us,
We must learn to live in the moment
And, if honesty can find us,
Then most of us seek atonement
What have we got, but for today?
And today we must choose to live it
If a tomorrow comes our way,
Then only the Lord will give it
Now, I cannot say what is true for you,
But I feel at least I should say this;

David Oldakowski

If you live in the moment, when you do
It shall be a moment you'll never miss
As you turn around and look behind you,
Expecting to see your tracks in the sand
You'll find they've washed away to remind you
The only place you should be is where you stand —

BEAUTIFUL MIND OF MINE

Oh, you, dear mind of mine…beautiful mind of mine
Analytically exotic, hyperactive and quixotic
What am I to do with you…oh, beautiful mind of mine?
You wake me in the morning before I wish to wake,
And me, from blissful dreaming,
you come too soon to take, Oh, beautiful mind of mine
Downloading information in a world that's gone astray
You are an inspiration in all that I do and say
Oh, beautiful mind of mine
Abiding in disillusionment is quite a place to be
My feelings all are so content in knowing
I am free Oh, beautiful mind of mine
There is no more disquietude perplexing to my mind
And I am full of gratitude for troubles left behind
And you, my beautiful mind,
Oh, beautiful mind of mine

David Oldakowski

BEGIN TO LOVE

In the vibrant chaos of selfish will
We fiercely yearn for harmony
And amid the screams of those we kill
We turn our hearts from empathy
What will it take for us to learn?
For us to finally discern
That we're not earthbound very long
That this is not where we belong
Our lives are but a gift to share
At home, at work and everywhere
Friends, please begin to love today
Before our lives are passed away!

BELIEVE IN YOU

If I were to believe in something
It would have to be believable
It would have to be tangible
It would have to have proof
If I were to believe in something
It would have to be worthy of my while
It would make me want to pursue it
It would cause me to get out of bed
If I were to believe in something
It would be worth my dying for
It would cause me immeasurable passion
It would make me feel love!
Well, I believe in you!

Bi-Polar

Well, it's A – okay
And such a merry-good thing
When everything
Goes my way
I get a chill inside
And I swell with pride
When good times
Are here to stay
Then all of a sudden
Something goes wrong
And I crash and burn
And I scream and cry
I lose the faith
That seemed so strong
And I feel I might
Lie down and die

Breakfast with the Enemy

Crouched and creeping through thorny, Loud and black anger –
The ever-twisting, Icy-wet roads of rage –
Never entertaining nor embracing It's colorless self-defeat -
As it lurks and stalks and Mills about my stage –
I thought I knew what hatred was Until I sat in its presence –
And felt the unyielding strength Of its suffocating glare –
I instantly began to pray as I Gathered up my breakfast tray –
And besought my awesome God to Spirit me away from there –

David Oldakowski

Can You Keep a Secret?

Seems like everywhere you go
We hear the people say
That secrets are not secrets lest
You give them all away
Hey you, my friend, come here,
And let me whisper in your ear;
I've got a secret, can you keep it?
Can you keep it if I tell you?
No matter what compels you,
I've got a secret, can you keep it?
No one keeps a secret anymore
It's terrible but true
They say to keep a secret seems
To be a bit taboo
A secret's not worth knowing
If you have to keep it to yourself
A secret drives you crazy
Till you can tell somebody else
I say a secret told in confidence
Is like a precious stone,
That should be hidden in a vaulted-safe
By the one you've told-alone

Yes, the world may say that secrets
Are just not sacred anymore;
Yet, if not a bond between close friends,
Then what else are secrets for?
Hey you, my friend, come here,
And let me whisper in your ear;
I've got a secret, can you keep it?
Can you keep it if I tell you?
No matter what compels you?
I've got a secret, can you keep it?

Coming Ashore

I sit here thinking and trying to write
Fighting my demons late in the night
I look at your picture and feel such regret
Then realize our lives are not over yet
The look in your eyes reminds me of times
As dear to my heart as are nursery-rhymes
It wasn't all bad between you and I
And there is still time before we both die
The love that we shared was so meant to be
And the future is not yet for us to see
My years of sailing will soon come to shore
And there'll be a day when I'll see you once more

Confession Session

Like twisted, tangled roots
Of a hundred-year-old tree
Are all the grievous sorrows
That haunt me ceaselessly So many hearts
I've won and lost Because of selfish need
Sometimes leaving in my wake
The virtue of my seed For, what better else
May a mortal human spawn
Than a product of his love
Before he's dead and gone?
I've asked myself a thousand times
Why the choices that I've made
Compelled to do only that
Which my inner voices bade
Through all those years of drinking
Unable to discern
"No man can serve two masters"
As I have come to learn
So, every night I beg of God
To free me of my guilt and shame
And every night I pray to God
In Jesus" Holy name

Designed by You

Just as fire's ignited by smoldering coal
It's the Holy Spirit that lights up my soul
But I'm still a man of flesh and bone
And I'm sick and tired of being alone
So forgive me, Lord, but I need some love
Which isn't provided there up above
My flesh is screaming for me to hear
That it needs a woman to hold it near
And my bones are aching for her touch
To the point I feel I'm dying for such
So Lord, please help me if you will
To ease my yearning just until
I can find the one you've chosen for me
To share with my life so faithfully
The woman You've groomed to be my bride
And the one in whose trust I may confide
For, just as you formed me from the dust
I know you can spare me suffering lust
And bless me instead with love that is true
The one made for me, and designed by You

Down to Business

"I Am" in this human body, a living (and dying) Fleshly
product of my alien ancestors This body is programed,
programed to keep itself alive; At any cost. Programed to
provide itself with nourishment and pleasure; At any cost.
Programed to seek love, affection and other Various forms of
social stimulation; at any cost – Programed to want and to
need acceptance and security In an unacceptable and insecure
world-era – Programed to fear that which is unknown; like
death, and life Programed to seek refuge
from the sorrows and pain of the present,
By sweet, nostalgic reminiscing in the multi-colored realm
Of a bitter-sweet, non-existent past. –
Yes, I dwell in this body for a moment in eternity; this body
Programed, programed by this world.
Yes, this body is pro- gramed by 60
Trillion cells and pre-recorded DNA –
I go a better way! You see, my friends,
I have programed enough! It is time now
For me to be about my father's business! The business of Really
living; the business of deep loving, and then of course,
The business of rightly dying.
Time to get down to business!

FEEBLE CONTRACT

Come, my friend, and take a drink
And I'll make you come to see -
That I will change the way you think
And give you new reality –
I'll make you happy instead of sad
And I'll take away your fears
I'll give you friends like you never had
As long as you buy them beers –
I'll give you cravings endlessly
And I'll teach you how to feed them –
I'll take away your family
Cause you'll no longer need them –
I'll take away what living brings
Like responsibility and grief –
I'll take away a lot of things
As I am the greatest thief –
Now, there is a charge initially
For all that I take and give –
And a total cost of dignity For as long as you may live –
Yes, for a one-time-only, unreasonable fee
I'll take away your pain and strife –
And if you'll loyally drink with me

*I'll even take away your life –
But, I'll be there to help them carry you
Upon the breath of your friends –
For, on the day when they bury you
That's when our contract ends –
Sincerely, Your Friend, Alcohol*

David Oldakowski

FOR MY WIFE TO BE

*Darling, your attitude reminds me
of a better place and time,
In a world back when people
were so generous and kind —
And, oh, your gratitude refines me,
love, like aged and precious wine —
I am better for the knowing of your open heart and mind! —
Your tenderness as you undress the secrets that I hold,
I realize that in your eyes is where I shall grow old —
Yet, until then, and thrice again,
I yearn to feel your warm embrace! —
Then we shall live our lives to give,
To God and His amazing grace! —*

GHOST RIDER

If only my car could speak,
All the stories it would tell –
All the sex in its back seat,
All the partying from hell –
All the drinking that we did,
Back when I was just a kid –
Driving late into the nights,
Getting high and picking fights –
Drinking booze and racing cars,
Getting laid beneath the stars –
Empty six-packs in the trunk,
Driving home so puking drunk –
That final night there in the rain,
I was murdered by a train –
My car survived but I did not,
I miss my friends an awful lot –
If I could go right back to then,
I'd never drink and drive again –
But I don't drive my car anymore,
I'm just a ghost rider of folklore –

David Oldakowski

God Is Grooming Us

Were you terribly hurt when he left you?
Did it feel like a thousand hot
daggers had pierced your heart?
Were you horribly hurt when he left you?
Did it feel like a demon had seized
your heart and tore it apart? –
Did you feel like you were
drowning in an ocean of tears?
And thought you'd die in the bed where you lay?
Did you cry all night and into the morning?
While praying God hears all of the words
That your heart had to say?
Did your friends all keep asking you
What ever was wrong?
As you smiled, said nothing And tried to be strong?
Did you quit your job?
And move out of town?
Then changed your mind when
Your plane had touched down?
Did you give up hope?
And pick up a drink?
To clear out your head and

To help you to think?
Did you finally get sick? And so tired of crying? –
That you finally took steps To see to your dying? –
Well…I did!
I did all of those things And I cried!
I did all of those things And I died!
I was terribly hurt When she left me!
And I felt like a Thousand hot daggers
Had pierced my heart!
I was horribly hurt When she left me!
And I felt like a Demon seized my life And tore it apart! –
Yes, I felt like I was drowning In an ocean of tears –
And thought I'd die in the bed where I lay! –
Yes, I cried all night and into the morning
While praying God hears –
All of the words
That my heart had to say! –
Yes, my friends all kept asking me
What ever was wrong –?
As I smiled, said nothing,
And tried to be strong! –
Yes, I quit my job
And moved out of town –
Then changed my mind when
My plane had touched down –
Yes, I gave up hope And picked up a drink –
To clear out my head And help me to think –

David Oldakowski

*Yes, I finally got sick And so tired of crying –
That I finally took steps To see to my dying! –
Well…I did!
I did all of those things And I cried! –
Yes…I did!
I did all of those things
And I died! –
But we're not the ones who decide! –
And this is how God replied…
"Child, if I am like you And you are like me
We know suffering And drinking –
Will not make us see! –
Child, if you are like me And I am like you
We know suffering And thinking
Is what we must do! –
For, it is by my will As you are coming
To learn –
That by suffering, my Word, you will Discern! –
For, it is by my will As you are coming To know –
That because you're my child I'm helping you grow!!"
Well, my love, My wife to be –
If I am like you And you are Like me –
Together we've learned So very clearly
That we are precisely As God wants us to be! –
For, if you are like me And I am like you –
And we keep on doing As God wants
Us to do –*

Nothing will take us off of His path –
And nothing will make us subject to His wrath –
Nor cause a blooming fuss! –
Let's allow God to take us into His care –
And I know He will make us become aware –
That He is grooming us! –

David Oldakowski

God, How I Love the Rain

Softly, steadily Rhythmically drumming –
Setting a mood
Taking me back –
Thunder-crashing cymbals –
The rain, oh Lord, how I love the rain –
The pain, the anger,
Punching and pounding
And screaming in rage –
Thrashing explosions
Of broken hearts
And loves gone bad –
The rain, oh Lord,
how I do love the rain –
The soft, misty drizzle
Of my tears –
The weather-beaten paintings Of my years –
The rain, oh God, how I love the rain –

Greater Things

I'm bound for greater things…
I'm struggling now but you will see,
Things will not get the best of me –
I'm bound for greater things…
When troubled times get in my way,
I dream about a better day –
I'm bound for greater things…
When the road I trudge seems far too long,
The good Lord makes me swift and strong –
I'm bound for greater things…
When life's' little problems stack up on me,
I pray to God for more energy –
I'm bound for greater things…
No matter what your case may be,
Things will get better and you will see,
You're bound for greater things! –

David Oldakowski

Grown-up Little Boy

Seems like just the other day…
I was told by society –
That I am a grown man now
And I should act with piety –
So, I am a grown man now
Exactly what I prayed to be –
When I was a little boy
And people were unsure of me –
I say, I am a little boy now
Though not the one I used to be For,
with no one now abusing me
I get to be the boy I choose to be –
If I am a grown man now
Letting go the pride in me –
I try to be that little boy
Who still, somehow, resides in me –
I'm a grown-up little boy now
And with just a touch of vanity –
As God is surely blessing me –
By giving me back my sanity –

Happy Mother's Day, Again

You gave me life, you gave me birth, And so much love upon
this earth — With your open arms and loving heart,
You gave this child a place to start —
You cleaned the mess when I made a spill, And you cared for me
when I was ill — You pushed me on the merry-go-round,
And picked me up when ere I fell down —
You made me PBJ's and chips for lunch,
And you showed me how to throw a punch — Then you taught
me how to read and write, And just how to say my prayers at
night — When I was weak you made me strong,
And always showed me right from wrong —
And when my life was hard to swallow,
You set good rules for me to follow —
With all things said, this much is true, You gave me the very
best of you — And when it came time for me to go, You stood
aside and you let me grow —
So accept my thanks, I wish you would,
Because you gave me everything you could —
Now in Jesus' name, for you, I pray,
You'll have a very "Happy Mother's Day!" —

Happy Mother's Day

Mere words alone cannot express
My deeply seated thankfulness –
That God appointed you my mother
Who stands in shadow of no one other –
They say "a mother's work is never done"
And I hope in our case this is true –
Cause you're a model for everyone
Just as the Lord intended for you –
So do not fret but be of good cheer
Continue to serve bread unleavened –
For a while longer you're needed here
And you've already earned your place in Heaven –

Here to Tell Them

Here in this prison it's become very clear
That here in this prison, Lord, You need me here! —
Here are the worst of the worst and the baddest of the
bad Those who are drowning of thirst and who've lost all
they had — They are hobbled and humbled and some are
way-mean men Cryin "please mamma please,
I won't do it again!" —
They're headed for hell, then, just as sure as their sin
Needing someone to tell them how and where to begin —
Now these are the babies who were born of their parent's
dope And these are the children who have been cheated
of their hope —
Victimizers and victims all one in the same
Who are lost in the system and losing the game —
So, am I here to tell them how to start life anew?
Yes, Lord, I'm here to tell them of the mercy of You! —
Here in this prison it's become very clear
That here in this prison, Lord, You need me here —
Yes, Lord, I'm here to tell them how to begin life anew
Yes, Lord, I'm here to tell them of the glory of You! —

I Cannot Wait

I say it's not enough anymore
Just knowing that you exist –
Finding you has become a thing
Upon which I must insist! –
Oh, love, will you feel it's me,
When I know that I have found you? –
Oh, love, will you know it's me,
When you feel my arms around you? –
I cannot wait to see
The look in your eyes
When you finally Come to realize,
That I'm the one God made for you,
And you're the one He made for me –
I cannot wait So share with you
The beginning of Eternity! –

I Do

I don't recall any dirty looks, only the
Playful smile of your lovely face –
I don't remember any hurtful words,
Nor any silly fussing and fighting,
I don't – I don't remember our holding grudges
Or getting even, nor seeking revenge,
I don't –
And I cannot bear the thought of your leaving me
I don't remember – I won't –
Because in your heart I knew that
I would always be there, I knew –
I do remember being lost (as you)
Deep within the soft, loving completeness
Of your passionate kisses –
This I do remember, yes, I do –

David Oldakowski

I Know Who You Are

When I came to this prison I was still immature,
I knew what your name was but not who you were –
But I slowly grew up and now I'm a man,
Because you were patient and you understand –
I needed some "time" just to figure it out,
And now I see clearly what you're all about –
When the sun goes down on that final day,
I'm gonna be needing a new place to stay –
When I walk through these gates for the very last time,
I'm gonna be leaving some good friends behind –
And when I start to pray, at the end of that day,
I'm gonna be searching for the right words to say –
All the pain and the suffering that I have been through,
Was well worth my while, cause it led me to you –
When I leave this old prison behind me for good,
I'm gonna be grateful that I understood –
All the time I've spent here has been worth it by far,
Cause now, my Lord Jesus, I know who you are! –

I Will To Surrender

I have lost my youthful innocents
Cause I had to face reality
That's why I chose to live within
The boundless realm of fantasy –
With health care costs and politics
Making our lives so hard to live
We find ourselves so deep in debt
And needing more than we can give –
While the Bible says that we should love
All of our neighbors as ourselves
We've got to care for our families
So we store up food upon our shelves –
We've built computers to rely on
Then blame them for our own mistakes
We've made our bed that we must lie on
And every day we raise the stakes –
So, I live my life inside my head
Logic making all my choices

David Oldakowski

To keep my heart from being broken
And my ending up hearing voices –
The gift of free will is dangerous
For, people lie and steal and kill
So I will myself to seek the
Lord Surrendering my own self will –

I Yield My Sword and Shield

*By fierce and passionate sorrow
I long to know true love
And to smell the flowers of its blooming bliss –
To bask in the throes of Love's innocents
And savor the fragrance of its mortal kiss –
My Lord, God, I pray thee
To grant me this true love
In all of its glory as I would perceive it –
Upon the wings of your
Fleece-covered angels and make me Lord,
worthy hence-forth to receive it –
From the blood-spattered battle-field Of mine heart
Where-upon lay my vanquished spirit –
I yield there my sword and my shield
With prayer and bow down
Before You and beg You to hear it –*

I'd Do It All Again

When I think of all the times you lied to me,
And then how I would always try to see
That you were only scared of what I might say —
I think you were only doing what you thought you had to do,
To keep me from doing something bad to you,
Like packing all my things to move away —
When I think of all the guilt you shoved on me,
Yet, how passionately you loved on me,
And all the efforts that we seemed to make in vain —
I realize all the tricks that you tried on me,
Before you actually died on me,
Have me now wishing that we could do it all again! —

IN A MOMENT

In a moment… You took yourself and
My daughter and you left me –
And for a very, very long time
I stopped living –
I existed day by day
Donning only the illusion of armor
I found in the consumption of
Weaker hearts than my own and alcohol –
In a moment…
Twenty years later, there you were
Kissing me and making love to me Once again –
All that sorrow and suffering behind us –
Then, in a moment…
You took yourself and
My daughter and you left me -

In Need of Me

Here I go again, again on the verge of tears
Listening to echoes which nobody else can hear –
She's dead and gone, but I just can't let her go
I try so hard but my progress is so slow –
I resent that we had never gotten married
And I don't even know where on Earth she is buried –
I feel the weight of the cross that Jesus carried –
I'm so sorry for all the times I made her cry Sometimes it makes
me wish that I'm the one who died –
I don't know what to do with all this heavy guilt
It's destroying all the good memories we built –
Oh Lord, I ask for your help in all of this
Please don't let me forget my loves' tender kiss –
Lord, help me to move on and set us both now free
I'm sure she's no longer in any need of me –
But I am, Lord, I am in need of me! –

INSPIRING PROMISE

I've ridden the tides of past accomplishments
about as far as I could
It's time to stand up and build new challenges
just the way a real man should –
Through all the clever and swank sales-
pitches which I had so well-rehearsed
And down the rivers of stank and deep ditches
all the muck that I traversed –
Around all the curves as they sharply bended
always leaving in my wake
Shattered dreams and hearts, some of them
untended moving on for more to take –
To celebrations and the black-tie dances
And the prizes won and lost –
Money and diamonds and sordid romances
Not all of it worth its cost –
If you do it wrong you'll have to pay
And you will never know just when –
Do a thing right the very first time
And you'll never have to do it again! –

It's All I Wanna Do

Your eyes sound like a romantic love letter
Your voice looks like a rippling mountain stream –
In fact, if I didn't know any better I'd say
you only exist within my dream –
All I wanna do is fall in love with you
Every single day
Like two children who've gone outside to play –
Like an aging couple whose hair is turning gray
All I wanna do is fall in love with you
Every single day –
I wanna fall in love with you again
On Monday and Tuesday –
And we'll set sail for the south of France –
Then fall in love with you again
On Wednesday and Thursday –
As we ride the golden wings of chance –
I wanna fall in love with you again
On Friday and Saturday –
And we will laugh and dance and sing –
Then fall in love with you again
Early Sunday morning
Thanking God for everything! –

All I wanna do is fall in love with you
Every single day –
Like two children who've gone outside to play
Like an aging couple whose hair is turning gray –
All I wanna do is fall in love with you
Every single day –

David Oldakowski

Jealousy and Envy

*It is as though I am watching
From the sidelines as others live My dreams –
I feel but a spectator full of jealousy
Watching the game of my life
Played out by strangers –
See the hero save the world, that's me
Fall in love and get the girl, that's me –
But all the while I realize
It isn't my reality –
I watch a mother and her child,
she Gives him reassurance -
Whilst I've been struggling all my life
Against this raging river's currents – Envy? –*

Kingdom City

Sometimes I speak before I think
When listening is the precious link –
Still nothing alters my honest feelings
And nothing persuades my human dealings –
For I shall tell the truth at any cost
And by this way no virtue's lost –
Now you may think that
I am weak Or that I know not what I seek –
Yet, I bid you, hold fast such thought
And ask yourself what you have sought –
Perhaps some riches, maybe fame
To be a victor in this life's game –
Perhaps you've sought the "perfect love"
The one of which we all dream of –
Well, no matter what your case may be
I offer this that you might see –
You and I are born to die
Though whilst we live and laugh and cry –
We take for granted our every breath
Yet, what do any of us know of death? –
Now a fellow Christian told me so
That these are things we all should know –

David Oldakowski

*We ask by living what do we gain
And feel that no one shares our pain –
We all know that life's not fair
Still our duty is our knowledge to share –
I wrote these words beneath a moon-lit sky
Hence I shall live before I die –*

Kissing Me

I didn't hear what you were saying
Until I started listening –
I didn't think I could love you again
Until you started kissing me –
I couldn't smell the flowers blooming
Nor could I hear the song of birds –
I couldn't feel the touch of Spring-time
Yet now I find I write these words –
For, now there's bird-song in my heart
And I see the Spring-time on your face –
And even though we're far apart
I smell your essence – just a trace –
Now I am listening to your voice
As it echoes deep within my tears –
And I have finally made the choice
To love you the rest of all my years –

Laugh At Me

Yes, "Hello!" Look up here at me I'm not much,
I'm not cool I'm here to be your fool —
You people look at me and laugh at me
And I used to take it personally —
But not anymore, not like before
I'm quick to say that it's ok
Cause the world needs more laughter —
I want to hear your laughter
Because I already feel your pain —
And I dance in your tears
Like I do in the rain
So please, yes and please
Let me hear your laughter! —

Learning to Learn

I pray today, Lord,
That I will open my mind
And let the Teacher teach me –
That by the power of Your
Holy Spirit Through Him
Your words will reach me –
Let me learn today not as
A man who thinks he knows,
But as a young child, Eager as he grows –

David Oldakowski

Limerick

Here I am in a prison now
Still so unsure of why and how –
How many more years
And sorrow-filled tears
Will my merciful God allow –?

Loud and Blissful Dreams

Loud and blissful dreams are happening to me
Of drums and tambourines, of cymbals and of strings –
Loud and blissful dreams of bells on ankle-bracelets
Worn by beautiful, barefoot belly-dancers
Scantily clad, and dancing all around me
Exuding the erotic essences of oils and perfumes
Candle-wax and incent smoke –
Loud and blissful dreams of joyful mirth and laughter
And singing in celebration of unity and love found
In the midst of warfare, here, on this dying planet of ours –
I awoke with a starving thirst to a silent, gray morning
A thirst quenched by consciousness
and a cool, comforting cup
Of nasty, state prison water –
I am sober again this day, at least this side of my dreams –
Loud and blissful dreams; I can still hear them and
I can still see and feel them and they're beckoning me –
Oh Lord, may I tarry just a little while longer
Here, and there, in these loud and blissful dreams? –

Love and Courage

I do not like reality, with all its hate and crime and greed
I fear it comes to prey on me, upon my weaknesses, to feed
I've spent my life a drinking-man,
to still my nerves and hold them back
To numb the pain of past regrets,
and give me courage which I lacked –
To face the world a sober man,
quite frankly scares me half to death
It cools the marrow in my bones,
and takes away my very breath –
I don't know where I lost my courage,
nor do I even know the cause
But I need to gain it back again,
just like the lion did in Oz –
I've got to get my courage back,
that fearless courage from my youth
Before I found out all the lies,
and back when I still knew the truth –
Well, Jesus loves me, this I know,
I knew this even from the start

I think He's the One who gave me,
that love and courage in my heart —
For, that the Bible tells me so,
I choose in this for to believe
When through this prison gate I go,
God's love and courage I'll receive —

David Oldakowski

LOVE CAN KILL

Love; it needs no explanation
For there are none that will make any sense –
And there is no reading of it
Nor even hearing of it
Which can equate its experience –
To feel it is the most
That one can hope for
And to lose it tis the great
Theme of most folklore –
You cannot speak reason to it
Nor expect a certain season to it –
For it comes and it goes as it will –
And though you may often cry about it
Perhaps even lie about it –
Love is the utmost reason to kill –

LOVES' PURE HAND

Upon the skyward wings of despair
Soaring through clouds of dismal gray –
You'll find my heart residing there
Perhaps forever where it shall stay –
Lord, as a king, a knight, or even a squire
I engage all battles honest and true –
By the sword of truth I would never tire
Yet a woman's demise had bid me ado –
Lord, a king, a knight, or squire I'm not
I am merely a noble, mortal man –
Still, for all the riches I haven't got
I would settle instead for loves' pure hand! –

MY AWESOME SAVIOR

I'm looking all around me And I see –
There are many people who're Much worse off than me –
I reckon I sure should be Grateful toward my Lord –
That I am still equipt to Wield His mighty sword –
I feel sadness And compassion –
For all those in Sickly fashion –
And I wish Although in vain –
That I could somehow Ease their pain –
So I shall look unto the west –
And do my very best –
To exhibit good behavior –
And serve my awesome savior –

My Charge in Prison

I look around me and I see, Anger,
hatred, suffering and shame –
Men whose lives are torn apart,
And who will never be the same –
This is a dwelling full of sickness,
Of souls who've lost their way –
And some will leave and live again,
But some of them will stay –
There are a few men just like me,
Who have gained by our mistakes –
Who will not come this way again,
And vowed, "no matter what it takes!" –
Yet, I see murderers and evil men,
And I am grateful they are here –
For, they're a few less dangers which
Our societies must fear –
So, when I'm called to cross their paths,
I'm charged with but one thing for to tell –
And that's the gospel of Jesus Christ,
Who will spare them from the gates of hell! –

David Oldakowski

My Children's' Eyes

With make-up, powder,
Rouge and blush,
At first she wore A good disguise –
But when she took Her war-paint off,
I found she wears
My children's' eyes –

My First Love Set Me Free

Now I cannot say by whom, though I know it has been said,
That we must pay our dues, in order to get ahead –
Life's no bed of roses; I know this to be true,
Still, by their thorns I bleed, sweet memories of you –
For, to love someone with all and everything you are,
Tis to bear the brutal pain of an ever-lasting scar –
And who could be so wise, so true enough to say,
That suffering inside of me would ever go away? –
Oh, the countless times I thought, I'd found somebody new,
Yet had to fight to stay myself from making love to you –
On those cold and rainy nights, I cried a timeless tear, Sharing
warmth with someone else, whilst wishing you were here –
Then once asleep I'd wake from dreams,
calling out your name,
Begging God to turn back time, and let things be the same –
Unending nights of sorrow, forever left me bound,
Causing me continually, to pursue my Savior's crown –
For, often I have wondered, yet never understood,
As mortal understandings are seldom any good –
So, with nowhere else to turn, and no one there to care,
I looked up to the sky, and gave my burden there –

David Oldakowski

For, a message sent to Heaven, upon the wings of a dove,
Shall bring back peace of mind,
to the heart that's pierced by love –
Well, all that was quite some time ago,
and today I do be- lieve,
The works of God are merely as great, as does one perceive –
For, surely it can only be, in answer to my prayers,
That I've found someone who's put to rest,
all my meaning- less affairs –
And who's replaced them in their stead,
with a love that is so true, -
It may only be compared by, that love I shared with you –
Yes, whether it is by faith or fate, I've found somebody new,
And when I'm making love with her, I no longer think of you
– On these cold and rainy nights, I've yet to shed another tear,
Instead I share her caring warmth,
whilst thanking God that she is here –
Once asleep I sleep and dream,
I dream of things to come to pass,
Like serenity eternally, and of a love that will forever last –
I'll not forget the night you died on me,
and God set your lovely spirit free,
And sometimes silent voices speak to me,
Saying, "never again shall I know love,
as I did with Stephanie!" –

But then one night I felt your voice,
as it softly spoke inside of me,
I listened closely as you whispered…
"I'll pray for you, please pray for me,
Now go, my first love set me free!" –

David Oldakowski

MY LOVE

My love is strong Stubborn Unrelenting –
Like the roots of a Redwood tree –
Those subterranean Ties that
Bind it – My love is long
Always Self-inventing –
If you sought to see Its ending
You would be quite Hard-pressed

To find it –

My Ministry of Poetry

Oh Lord, MY God, I come to thee
With humble heart on bended knee –
To ask in prayer so fervently
That thou will come and speak with me –
Of all the gifts you've given me
From sorrow to tranquility –
The one I cherish most would be
My ministry of poetry –
When Mother first gave birth to me
Although I came so painfully –
She cried aloud quite joyously
That I was here this world to see –
The system started testing me
And said I might be a prodigy –
They tried to steal my sanity
And binded my humanity –
I knew of Jesus basically
Yet nothing of eternity –
So as I came to know of thee
I prayed for You to rescue me –
As I grew older graciously
And learned of man's hypocrisy –

David Oldakowski

And rumors of conspiracy
I feared I'd lost my dignity –
With such a short expectancy
And knowledge of mortality –
I came to know eventually
My spiritual identity –
Now I am Yours so totally
So please make Your own use of me –
And thank You for my ministry
My ministry of poetry –

My Secret Wish

I want to hear the words I love you
And know that you really mean it
To admire the sky above you
And know that we've really seen it –
I want to share with you our plans and dreams
Take your hand and walk that sandy beach
I want to know you know how much it means
To persevere goals within our reach –
I want you not to mind if I act nuts
And for you to want to play along
For us to show courage and lots of guts
To conquer challenges so bold and strong –
But I don't want to want nor even try
To change the person you really are
You see, whilst we admired that beautiful sky
T'was you whom I wished for upon that star –
Oh, the rings and vows we will exchange
In our future not hence a-far
For you are the one who need not change
I love you just the way you are –
You are my wish upon a star –

My Soul-Self

Alive was I long before
The November day of my last birth –
Often I've passed through the timeless door
Affixed between Heaven and the earth –
I hold that this life which I now live
Is one in part of one to go –
For, I have so very much love to give
And worlds of things to come to know –
Yea, though I'm bounding forth by my choosing
In search of truth and of fairness –
And though mortal body I am loosing
I am gaining self-awareness –
Yea, I've come to know about my whole-self
Which exists beyond my flesh and bone –
Yea, I've realization of my soul-self
Which is destined to Heaven upon a throne –

New Life Begins

Though I cannot earn My way to Heaven –
I don't even deserve To build these stairs –
In Mark fifteen and Verse thirty-seven –
You'll find the reason
I proclaim my prayers –
For, t'was by His death –
Oh, the path He paved –
With His final breath –
Oh, that I am saved! –
For, when we ask forgiveness –
Of all our mortal sins –
We square away our business –
And our new life begins! –

David Oldakowski

No One like Jesus

He's the gracious one who frees us
From the debt of sin we owe –
And there's no one else like
Jesus In all the world we know –
No, there's no one else who sees us
The way we truly are –
And there's no one else like
Jesus The bright and morning star! –

Nothing Else

Those truthful lies told to me
In passions' realm of velvet dark –
Come across so differently
With morning's song of Meadowlark –
I close my eyes, feel the kiss
And ponder love's confusing way –
For, love is kind at first glance
If we see it in the light of day –
Tis when we look way too hard
To see with hearts of loneliness –
We find ourselves wondering how
We've come to be in such a mess –
So, do not search anymore
To find the love that should find you –
Lest you learn then in your quest
That nothing else will ever do –

David Oldakowski

Now Can Be Eternity

*Yesterday's dead and tomorrow's unborn
So there's nothing to fear and nothing to mourn –
For, all that has passed and all that has been
Can never return to be lived ere again –
And what lies ahead or the things that will be
Are still in our hands for eternity –
To live in the future is our great unknown
Though past and present we claim for our own –
Yet, all we need do is live for today
God will show us the truth and the way –
It's only the memory of things that have been
And expecting tomorrow to bring trouble again –
That fills our today, which we want to bless
With uncertain fears and borrowed distress –
All we need live for is this one little minute
For, life's here and now, and eternity's in it –*

Of Numerous Kinds

Looking at this photo of Mom and Dad
Taken by my brother just this year –
I think of all the problems we've had
Only to find ourselves standing here –
Standing here feeling so tired and vexed
Nursing our wounds from battles we've fought –
Each of us wondering, "What will come next?"
And will we succeed in the time that we've got? –
For, life is quite short, as we've all come to know
And we've seen how quickly time can pass by –
They say, "we get wiser the older we grow"
But will we find answers before we die? –
Well, I've asked the Lord to care for us all
To work in each of our hearts and minds –
And I pray with faith that He'll answer my call
And give us blessings…of numerous kinds! –

One Perfect Portrait

Like snowfall in Aspen
Brings me warm by a fire –
You've caused me to raise all
My standards much higher –
You're such a pure and
Pleasant attraction
Like a treasured memory
Or a loving embrace –
A perfect portrait
Of blissful distraction –
From all the perils
Of this human-race –
You've nourished my hunger
By feeding me first –
Whilst you stilled my cravings
And vanquished my thirst –
You have championed my heart
And commanded my awe –
By wielding compassion
Without any flaw –
Like rainfall in London
Brings me thoughts of romance –

*You've given me faith that
I may still have this chance –
You're such a kind and
Noble persuasion –
A humble reminder
Of all that is true –
A perfect portrait
Of timeless occasion –
To glorify my Discovery of You –
You gave me forgiveness
For wrong I have done –
And ended my searching
As You are the One –
You're the One I have sought
In the midst of my strife –
To love and to honor
For the rest of my life –*

David Oldakowski

OUR EARTH

Will it survive its injuries?
Tell me, how can it? –
Or is ours' a badly damaged
And dying planet? –
For, it lives and it breaths
As do all life-forms upon it –
And it warrants the glory
Of Shakespearian sonnet –
We belong to our earth just
As she belongs to us –
And it's time we, in her defense,
Stand up and raise a fuss! –
For, collectively, we shall be heard
Where-as alone, we sure may not –
We must not fail to save our earth
For, in this life, she's all we've got! –

Pleasant Premonition

Today, sometime round the hour of noon
It came for me to realize –
That I could be leaving this planet soon
Aboard the Christ-ship Enterprise –
For, some unique things have happened to me
Which seem to make some eerie sense –
And of which have left me excitedly
Expecting revelation hence –
As if a part of "Grand Design"
Or perhaps a puppet on a string –
I have been forced now to resign
Myself and will to greater things –
Though I am still seeking the perfect wife
And mortal success within this realm –
I've realized that God is ruling my life
And I am no longer manning the helm –
Yes, God is plotting my course up ahead

David Oldakowski

*While paving my pathway day after day –
So, in the event that I may soon be dead
Let it be known that I loved all the way –
And if by chance someone's reading all this
I'm asking you please whoever you are –
Give someone you love a hug and a kiss
And know God's with you wherever you are! –*

PLEASE TELL ME

I want to write another song
And one that folks can sing to –
But my words all seem to come out wrong
And sorrow's what I cling to –
Like nasty, old, green and yellow snot
And decaying and dying rot - Don't think I'm on the
"Pity-pot" That isn't my case, no, it's not –
No, I am just a deep young man
Struggling so hard to understand –
Just what it is that God wants from me
And how more lowly can I be –
For, what but death is victory?
In all this suffering that we see –
And who can tell a truth to me
Who has not died and been set free –
Tell me, please, tell me
Please, tell me –

David Oldakowski

Pondering P-Words

Perpetual penance perseveres,
Previous perceptions press –
Potential perils precipitate,
Puncturing precocious prowess –

Pray and Get Out of His Way

There is no more ugliness inside of me
But there's still a great deal of work to be done –
Only God knows how hard I've tried to see
That His work in me has already begun –
If I can just learn to get out of
His way Perhaps there's a chance I'll figure it out –
And rather than just struggling day after day
I believe He'll free me of fear and doubt –
Yes, if I just pray and get out of His way
I believe He will help me recover –
Yes, if I just pray and get out of His way
A whole new life He'll help me discover –
So, I'll just pray and get out of His way And,
in the sacred name of Jesus I pray – Amen –

David Oldakowski

Precious Acquisition

Slowly, many nights have come,
And just as slowly gone away –
Taking of my spirit some,
They've left me standing here today –
Wondering where that feeling's gone,
And if I'll get it back one day –
Springtime blossoms, summer's rain,
As Heaven's bursting up above –
Quenches all the fires of pain,
And all the fears that I think of –
I'm reminded once again,
That I have known the joy of love! –
In all the world I know,
Worthy of most recognition –
As the older we all grow,
And claim our disposition –
We all must labor and sow,
Life's most precious acquisition –

Problem Solver

Well I cannot speak for you,
but I hate to be wrong –
It isn't that I want always to be right,
I just despise being wrong! –
I hate to be wrong according to
Romans 7:14 – 25
In the scriptures of the Holy Bible –
Sure, some people think it would be great
to be right all the time –
As for me, I disagree.
If I were to be right all of the time,
there would be nothing
To challenge or to fix, and we as human
beings are problem solving machines –
We are designed to investigate and plot,
to experiment and research
To intend and to mend, to despair and repair,
to question and to answer,
To seek and to find – Yes, we are a species,
(Though some less or more equipt than others,)
Divinely designed to solve problems –
We are problem solvers –

David Oldakowski

Quiet Night

*It's a soft Quiet night—
No gunshots No sirens
Nor screams —
It's a quiet night —
A gentle breeze
Dancing with the drapes
No more pain than usual
I'm grateful for this fact —
It's a quiet night and
I am able to enjoy it
To embrace it —
I appreciate this night,
this Soft and quiet night —*

Rockin' for Freedom

Well, excuse me ladies and gentlemen too,
But I've got a few words I'd like to say to you —
I don't dance like Michael, can't sing like Price,
But I'm the badest white-boy you've seen since! —
You see, my name's not known from coast to coast,
And I don't give a damn about no breakfast toast —
Cause the importance of that is really quite small,
But what I've got to say concerns us all —
I'm talkin' bout life and how hard it is,
Cause the President thinks what's ours is his —
Unemployment puts our women on the pill,
While he picks his teeth with a hundred-dollar bill —
Now if you don't like what I've got to say,
There isn't anybody gonna make you stay —
You're free to leave if you think you should,
But if you can hang, I sure wish you would —
Well, I'm not you now, and you're not me,
And even though you may disagree —
I'm here to try to help you come to see,
That we're killing ourselves, yes, you and me —
By sitting back instead of taking a stand,
Against the angry old men who rule our land —

They hate our ways and this song I wrote,
But they're in power cause we don't vote –
So, I tell you now that the time is here,
Cause I feel that the end is getting near –
For us to come together, the new generation,
Trade the booze and drugs for indoctrination –
And to let it be heard that we're one big band,
Rockin' for freedom throughout our land! –
Now, I think it's time we stop ignoring these things,
And start ringing the bell for freedom that rings –
Have we lost our minds, as though it may seem,
And given up on the American dream? –
Can you hear what I'm saying, can you relate,
Cause if you think you can, then it's not too late! –
They forget about us, the old men don't care,
Cause we do drugs and grow long hair –
They outlaw pot and then sell us on booze,
So we will drink away our own right to choose –
Then they talk about peace cause they want to retire,
While they make more bombs and raise our taxes higher –
You see, we live in a time of drugs and sex,
And computers to make life more complex –
And with whips and chains and sexual tools,
Making love's become a silly game for fools –
So we cry inside when we ponder these things,
And finally see the outcome they will bring –
Cause when in this life there's no more love around,

We might just as well be dead in the ground –
Now our political games spell nuclear war,
But when the bombs go off there'll be no score –
We're all gonna lose, the young and the old,
And who will believe when the story is told –
About a whole world that gave up on love,
And turned its back on the Lord above –
Then fired these bombs out from their shell,
And sent them all right straight to hell? –
So like it was in the 60's with the flower-child,
When they all made love and let their hair grow wild –
Make love, not war, as they used to say,
And I, for one, would like to live that way –
And now, here it is, the bottom line,
It will be a better world for yours and for mine! –
So I say again that the time is here,
Cause I feel that the end is getting near –
For us to come together, the new generation,
Trade the booze and drugs for indoctrination –
And to let it be heard that we're one big band,
Rockin' for freedom throughout our land! –
Yes, we're rockin' for freedom, throughout our land! –

Searching

For all Of my life
I have Sought And fought To find
The kinds Of minds
Who've sought And fought
With thoughts The likes
Of which I do –

Shades of Gray

Like black and white is life and death
With shades of gray seen in between –
Before we take our final breath
We pray we have some color seen –
Like the serpent sheds its worn-out skin
We live for death which is our birth –
Yea, we die to live and pray to win
Some honest love and false self-worth –
The sun arrives to bring forth life
Whilst the moon goes down with mornings' light –
We find ourselves in pain and strife
In shades of gray and black and white –

David Oldakowski

Somewhere She Awaits Me

I've no idea what your name is
Nor how you look or where you live –
But I've faith in God that you exist –
I've no idea what your game is
Nor what you take
Or what you give –
But I won't be able To resist –
I've no idea where you are
Nor what you do or where you go
But I know that you are part of me –
Like a shining star
Where the north winds blow
You await my destiny –

Spare No Arrows

When darkness falls Upon my head
And I'm drowning in
The tears I've shed — I shall pray to God
To comfort me
Until the day when He rescues me —
And I will spare no arrows Until that day
When my father comes To take me away —
Yes, I'll keep on fighting
Every step of the way
And I'll spare no arrows Till dead I do lay —
Till ravens and sparrows Appear to me
I'll spare no arrows Until I am free —

Spiritual Development

With teardrops and coffee-stains I fill up each page
With music and growing-pains and passion and rage –
So, with all of my being I continue to write
Of all that I am seeing and with no end in sight –
But once I was willing to repent
then on and on and on it went
I became certain and confident of my
spirit's new development –
I've made some amazing discoveries in a
world that's quite a mess
And I know you have your ow
n worries but of this I must con- fess –
I have come to learn some astounding
things by admitting I don't know
And I can't express the joy it brings as
I witness myself grow! –
It is upon the wings of gratitude with
faith and hope that I ride

*Ever mindful of my latitude tis toward
Heaven that I glide –
It is not the things of this world
I seek for they shall only come to pass
Tis of the kingdom of Heaven
I speak for there my life shall forever last! –*

David Oldakowski

Stand Beside me Still

Like a soldier on the battlefield,
as though I've gone away to war,
I have armed myself with sword and shield,
prepared to even out the score —
For, deep within these prison walls,
where blood and hatred are abound,
I shall not fear when duty calls,
to lay my foes upon the ground —
Yet, when the evening comes to me,
and I'm alone here with my thoughts,
It is your heart I clearly see,
the hardest battle I have fought!
I know that I have wounded you,
by making choices that were wrong —
I pray you will forgive me, true,
and stand beside me all along? —
For, I shall face this as a man,
and I will take the weight that's due,

*But I just hope you'll understand
there'll be no victory with- out you! —
Please, write to me and let me know,
that you will stand be- side me, still,
This is my heart to you I show,
sincerely from your
"Little Will"*

David Oldakowski

Stiff Drink?

Oh, the temporary Comfort of Oblivion,
Brought on by A few cold, Stiff drinks –
But, oh, the
Adverse consequences
Brought on by
A few cold, Stiff drinks –

STILL LIVING

If only you could see me now you'd see
I'm different than before
I do for others all that I'm able, and
I'm not so selfish any- more –
If only you could hear me now,
you'd hear me sing a brand- new tune
I speak of love and joy and peace,
instead of crying my life in ruin –
If only you could feel me now,
you'd feel I've so much love to give
I'm opening up my heart and mind,
and I'm relearning how to live –
If only you could touch me now,
you'd touch the man you once dreamed of
For God has freed me of this flesh,
and filled my spirit with His love –
If only you could be here now,
although I know you never will
You'd be my wife as we had planned,
if only you were living still –

David Oldakowski

STILL SEARCHING

How is it that I Find myself Anticipating Breath –
While contemplating Death? –
How is it that I Find myself Contemplating Breath –
While anticipating Death? – How is it
That I Find… Myself? –

Tarnished Armor

*Perhaps I lived another life,
where I was envied and de- spised,
So I wear this mortal body,
in which I'm cleverly disguised –
I think I came from royalty,
seeking justice where-ere I could,
I swore an oath of loyalty,
upon the throne for which I stood
I fought against the anarchy,
which threatened to destroy our land,
I strove instead for liberty,
sure that united we would stand –
I pledged my life to serve these things,
as any noble knight would do,
And prayed to hear how victory sings,
before my valiant reign was through –
Yet, evil forces stole my crown,
and took my kingdom for its own,
And in the blood-shed I was drowned,
the worst defeat I'd ever known –*

David Oldakowski

*Now, I've been given one more chance,
to find the lost, where-ere they dwell,
To conquer evil with God's lance,
and rescue all our souls from hell! –*

That Small Boy

I miss the ways of innocence
Not knowing what's to come –
No guilt within my sub-conscience
For wrong things I have done –
I miss that boy who's part of me
So pure, so good and true –
Now, have I lost my dignity
In what I've said to you? –
I want to know that boy again
Who used to live inside –
Before the world hurt him, then,
He ran away to hide –
I'm looking for him, day by day,
I feel that he is near –
I want him to come out and play
And put away his fear –
I want to show him life brand-new
And share with him some joy –
So please, Lord, see what you can do For,
I am that small boy –

David Oldakowski

The Good Things

*A playful dog wagging its tail
A child discovers his shadow –
A blooper on the radio
Or a skirt giving way to a breeze –
A fish that jumps near my bobber
A mistake I made in public –
A smile pointed in my direction
Or a thought of something funny –
A foal on wobbly knees
A kitten, well, just being a kitten –
A soft drizzly rain-storm
Or a brilliant, quiet snowfall –
These are the things that make me smile
These are the good things in my life –*

THE HOLY SPIRIT WHISPERS...

There, in the shadows,
I can hear Whispers
In wind-swept swirls —
They ask…
Did I have a chance today
To be a friend,
And didn't take it? —
Or to make a choice Toward a
Better end,
And couldn't make it? —

David Oldakowski

THE NATURE OF A WOMAN

*One of my fiercest passions in life has been that of
Engaging, and even challenging,
the true nature of A female's emotions –
Because, as a man, I think
I understand that In order to truly respect a rose, –
I must first be able to understand the very
Nature of the root
From which it grows –*

THE NATURE OF MY SOUL

Love… is the very Substance of my nature –
Free… as a fragrant Summer's breeze –
Fierce… as the typhoon's Raging seas –
Long…as the endless Desert sands –
Soft… as a new-born Baby's hands –
Brave… as a gallant Soldier's sword –
Just… as the likeness Of my Lord –
To love… is the very Nature of my soul –

David Oldakowski

The Other Day

I thought of you
The other day
The way you are
The things you say –
And for that moment
The other day
All my worries
Went away –
So I just came by
To see you and say
That when I saw you
Again today –
It made me think
Of the other day
When I thought of you
And forgot to say –
I love you, darling,
Right now today –

The Track Back to Me

Whenever I feel insecurity
I go get lost in obscurity
With no one to answer to and nothing
I have to do I rediscover my purity –
Sometimes I go drinking, always
I am thinking And again I rediscover me –
Sometimes I go wandering, always
I am pondering Exactly what my next move will be? –
And then, when love has found me,
by the people who surround me
And their love begins to turn me around
upon my journey It never ceases to astound me –
Now, one day I'll arrive there and
learn how to survive there
In that place I've so long sought to be –
And when I do I'll surely look back down
this rugged, lone- some track,
Which is taking me where I want to be,
and I'll see That it brought me back to me! –

David Oldakowski

The Ways of Good

Iniquity and vengeance Is not my turn to go –
Lest I would have to sacrifice
The good I've come to know –
Vanity and arrogance
Are useless ways of thought –
And will in time prevent you from
Achieving goals you've sought –
I choose to turn to kindness
And all the ways of good –
For, anything less is mindless
And way misunderstood –

Those of Us

If by chance Perhaps you may Listen to
The words I say –
Then I believe You'll come to see
The valiant soul Inside of me –
And if you'll look Without your eyes
In time you'll come To realize –
We're not so different After all
All those of us Who heed God's call –
We're a lot alike In fact you see
And Heaven is Our destiny –

To Love Again

Like autumn strips tree's branches bear
And leaves them naked standing there –
You found my secrets where they hide
And conquered all my useless pride –
Then winter came by North winds' chill
And left all waters freezing…still –
You broke my heart and went your way
And left me suffering to this day –
But just as Earth awaits the spring
When flowers bloom and birds will sing –
I know I'll vanquish all this pain
And I shall live…to love again! –

To Pen My Final Page

Something ails me, my Lord;
I live in continuous fear,
I see hateful actions all around me,
and I feel your vengeance drawing near –
Lord, I do not wish to die in vain,
by the hand of evil's wan- ton rage,
Lest what has all my strife been for
if not to pen a final page? –
Oh Lord, I fret I've lost your courage,
the rugged sight of my mortal quest,
And nowhere do I feel like I belong. –
And Lord, my body suffers damage;
I live in constant pain and unrest,
And there's no more reason to be strong –
I feel my body dying slowly whilst
I struggle to live through one more day,
I long for love and yet all the while my
passion for love is fading away –
So well-rehearsed I play all the roles,
a wretched actor upon my own stage,
As for this play which I write,
I live for the day I shall pen my last page –

David Oldakowski

True Friend

*Just a memoir here to say
I'm glad you are my friend today —
There were many years
I hadn't the nerve (Nor did I deserve)
To have a true friend
Because I wasn't a true friend —
Now, thanks to God
And people like you
Who've helped me open my heart's doors
I thank you, friend, for being my friend
And allowing me to be yours —*

Unlovable

How foolish I was To think
That I was in control –
How weak I was
In my disillusionment –
How imperceptible Was my fear
That you would see right through me –
How could I have believed
That you honestly loved me
When I thought I was Unlovable –

David Oldakowski

Unmasked Sorrow

I may say that I hold power
That I am in control
Though I create Not the flower
Nor do I the New-born foal –
I may say that I'm intelligent
A gifted soul of choice Yet, none of this
Is relevant
As I listen to a voice –
A voice upon a magic plane
Suspended like a kiss
A voice that speaks
In tragic wane
Impending soul's a-miss –
So, as I look upon the morrow
Conversing with my friend
My love tis unmasked sorrow
Rehearsing till my end -

WE GIVE OUR CHILDREN

We're here for a moment
Then we're gone
And who will Remember us then? –
If not for the children That we spawn
Who will know
That we've ever been? –
So give to these children
Oh yes, and love them –
Put nothing ever
Else above them –
For, as we grow old
And approach the grave –
All we take with us
Is that which we gave –

WHAT DO YOU SAY?

Some say that rules are meant to be broken
That lies are acceptable if they're honestly spoken –
That dreams are for dreamers who cannot succeed
And romance will cut you and laugh as you bleed –
That we should be grateful for things which we're not
And a man is entitled to all that he's got –
That hearts will mend with the passing of time
And our human condition is our greatest crime –
That it isn't our fault this life is unfair
And living is useless and full of despair –
Well, I say that rules are to guide us along
And our lies are evil, hurtful and wrong –
That dreams are goals for which we strive
And love with romance shall keep us alive –
That we should be grateful for the things we learn
And we're only entitled to that which we earn –
That our hearts will heal when we choose to forgive
And we're only human for as long as we live –
That fault belongs only to those who blame it
And Heaven awaits us as soon as we claim it –

WHAT EVER HAPPENED?

What ever happened to Mom and Dad?
And the little ones at play on the swing? —
What ever happened to the morals we had?
For today they don't mean a thing? —
Our fathers fought in a world at war
To make certain our country free —
Yet freedom's become a tool of the whore
And the buyers have no dignity —
You see, when love does turn to hate
And turn it may so easily — We come to see a bit too late
That it's not what love's supposed to be —
Oh, we chance our love on wedding-day
Yea, submit on satin pillow's rest —
Then tears of love upon bedding lay
As another heart concedes the quest —
We start to hate what love has done
And hate ourselves for letting it be — We ask ourselves
what we have won By finding love then setting it free —
Yes, what ever happened to husband and wife?
And having children to adore? —
What ever happened to the meaning in life?
Is it lost forever more?

David Oldakowski

When Raindrops Fall

Whenever raindrops fall
And alight upon
God's supreme creation –
It brings forth a
Clean, fresh feeling inside me
Lacking explaination –
The way the wind Blows a cool, soft,
Whispering breeze – One that howls
And swirls Through the branches
Of the swaying trees –
The way the soil moistens
And enriches itself with
The fresh-fallen rain –
And the old tribal rhythms It creates as it
Pitters and patters upon
My window-pane – Yes, Lord, as I listen,
Whenever raindrops fall – I can hear the
Angel's voices call Telling me that all
And all is well
Whenever raindrops fall –

(Written in 1972)

When Things Go Wrong

When something happens in my life
That hurts me very much –
I go to God to comfort me And seek His loving touch –
I tell Him exactly what's gone wrong And ask Him, then, for
His advice – And though His answers may be long
They always seem to be concise –
He gives me strength to deal with things That, alone,
I cannot seem to bear – And, oh, the awesome joy it brings
To know that He is always there! –
So, I say, "Thank You," to my Lord
Each and every trying night – And pray that,
by His own accord I will wake with morning's light –

David Oldakowski

When You Need It

People can be so mean to you
Though it's not what they mean to do –
Every time we turn around
Someone's there to let us down –
Smile into our believing eyes
Telling only deceiving lies –
But God is always there for you
To let you know He cares for you –
Yes, if you've a hunger He will feed it –
And He'll give you courage When you need it –

WHY ME, LORD?

Lord, you must have had a reason
For placing me here on Earth –
Some purpose there in your season
For giving to me my birth –
But as I stand here looking back
On all that I've done so far –
I find myself unworthy of Even knowing who you are –
I'm such a lowly sinner who, Can't possibly deserve you –
A looser, not a winner who, Can qualify to serve you –
Why me, Lord? –
Please tell me, Lord, Why is there me? –

Without Crying

When the sound of the music is all out of tune
And even the wrong words still seem to rhyme
Like pale pastel-colored weddings in the month of June
To write a sad song without crying seems to me like a crime
When my heart is broken and I want to express it
And my conscience tells me to try to repress it
I can't seem to find a place to begin
As I fight a battle I don't want to win
To sing a sad song without crying seems to me like a crime –
How can anyone truly feel my pain
Unless I find a way to let them own it
What else is there in our lives to gain
If we've never felt sorrow nor even known it
To sing a sad song without crying seems to me like a crime –

Write You Right into My Life

When I wrote these words way back when,
it all seemed like a fantasy -
But now you're reading them again,
cause that's the way it was meant to be —
Like a hundred times, and maybe more,
I've tried to tell you these things before, -
And I'm not sure why nor even how,
but something has made me wait till now —
Living in darkness it was all I could do, -
To pray to the Lord that He'd lead me to you —
And when the risen Son gave me His light, -
I decided to write you right into my life —
You see, more than air, or even life itself,
I love you more than anything else -
And I think I'll die of a broken heart,
if you won't give us a chance to start —
Yes, I think I'll die of a heart-attack,
if you are unable to love me back -
Of all the beautiful words I know and all the feelings
I'm scared to show —

David Oldakowski

Well, now I'm saying these words for true,
and sharing these feelings with only you -
Living in darkness it was all I could do, -
To pray to the Lord that He'd lead me to you —
And when the risen Son gave me His light, -
I decided to write you right into my life —
So sudden as it may very well be,
it is of the utmost necessity,
-
As you can quite probably clearly see,
I'm trying to ask you to marry me? —

You Belong With Me

Like fat green frogs And great chili-dogs
And tough little boys And their Tonka-toys –
You've got to see…
Like yuppies and maybes And puppies and babies
And passion and glory And sad love stories –
You've got to see…
Like rain and snow And wine and song
You've got to know That you belong –
Yes, you've got to see That you belong
You belong with me -

David Oldakowski

You Keep Me Whole

I looked outside the other day
And saw the leaves had blown away —
I looked inside my heart today
And found that love was here to stay —
I thought I would die When you left me here —
Alone and crying
And full of fear —
Yet the powerful love
You left behind —
That one wonders of But seldom finds —
I hold it here Within my soul —
For it gives me joy
And keeps me whole —

Your Champion Awaits

Woman, I say to you…
Though my armor is a bit
Tattered and tarnished
By this mortal incarnation
From its very start –
I am still a noble knight
And only honor
And integrity reside Within my heart –
So let me, I pray thee,
Champion you away from there
With me, upon the back
Of my trusty steed –
And I will provide
For you most of all
That you may want, and all
Of that which you most need –
So take up your heart
Your hopes and your dreams
And approach the open gates –
For, with the Lord God at
My back I say to you, Woman,
Your Champion Awaits –

YOUR FACE I HOLD IN ME

*At this particular point in time, so vulnerably
I find That my flesh is fighting against my mind –
And though I forfeit my own false pride,
My heart is on my fleshes' side –
I want you in my arms, yet I barely know your name,
My passion longs to show you a wild you cannot tame – This
fury that I feel inside, may cause my heart to burst, But not to
taste your body's wine, I'd rather die of thirst –
I crave to stroke your golden hair,
and ravage all your private space,
And whilst I close my eyes tonight,
tis my dream to hold your face –*

YOUR FINAL DAY

But we just couldn't see the forest
For all of the trees that were in our view –
I find myself still in that old forest
Mingling in memories of my love with you –
You made it so hard for me to stay
Before you made me go away –
And we just couldn't see the sunlight
For all of those trees that got in our way –
No we could not see the sunlight
Before you lived your final day –

David Oldakowski

Your Secret Lies

From the murky, vacant depth of my heart
I bring these words to you –
And I pray to God you'll care for me
Some day before our lives are through –
You see, every time I look at you
I feel your essence all around me –
I admire the texture of your skin
And feel my own as it surrounds me –
And each time that you talk to me
Your voice is music to my ears –
Like the Philharmonic orchestra
Your words will echo through my years –
Every time that I've been near you
I feel all my senses come alive –
And I find myself looking forward
To the next time you arrive –
Although you may not know it
I can see a sadness in your eyes –
And it makes me want to comfort you
There, where-in your secret lies –

Your Victory in Me

Hate me now and love me later
And that'll be okay with me –
My love for you is even greater
Than greatness will ever be –
You cannot measure my love for you
It just isn't a thing to be done –
Forget all the things you ever knew
And every place beneath the sun –
Then you'll glimpse my loves' domain
And all the places it can reach –
You'll see the weight my love can sustain
And all that it has to learn and teach –
If you will open your heart to me
I'll fill you up from deep within –
In me you'll find your victory
And a brand new living to begin –

Love Jesus

David Oldakowski

Your Victory

*You have probably heard me say
That I want a lot of things –
Like everything to go my way
And the pleasure that this brings –
But more than anything else
I really want to be –
My father's most important Legacy –
And I pray to God That you, through me,
Will grasp your greatest*

Victory –

www.ingramcontent.com/pod-product-compliance
Lightning Source LLC
LaVergne TN
LVHW021048100526
838202LV00079B/4831